Your Own BIG BED

by **RITA M. BERGSTEIN**

pictures by **SUSAN KATHLEEN HARTUNG**

VIKING

Crack! Baby chick cracked out of his shell.

Peck! Push! Baby alligator pecked a hole in his shell.

Chip! Chip! Baby sea turtle grew too big for her shell.

And you grew and grew until you were
too big for your mother's tummy.

Soon they all came out—

and so did you!

This little koala bear was carried on his mother's back.

This baby kangaroo rode in her mother's pouch.

Mother tiger carried her cub in her mouth.

And you were carried everywhere, too.

Soon they all took their first steps—

and so did you!

After learning to fly, this bird sleeps in her comfy nest.

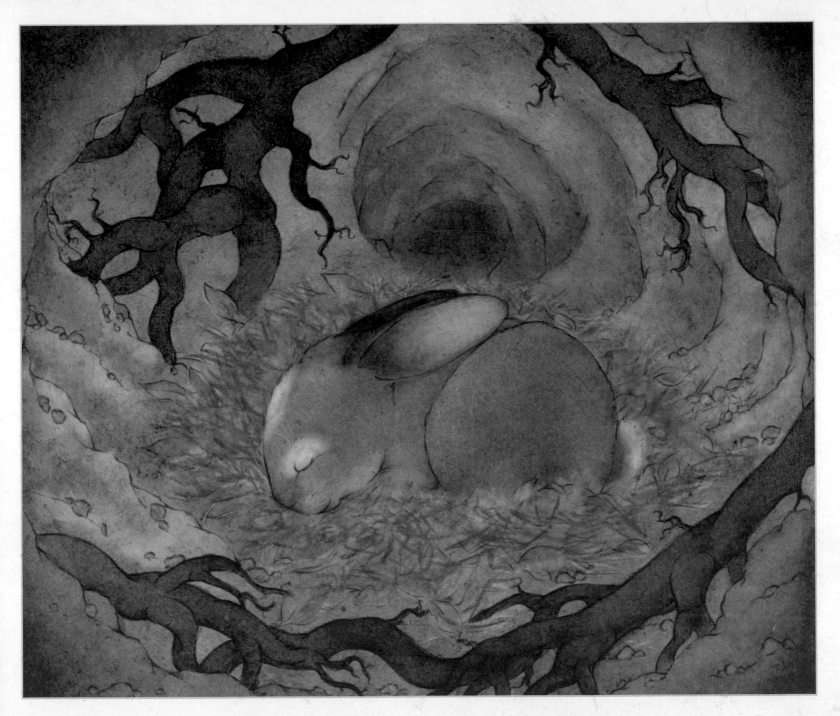

After hopping in the meadow,
this bunny naps in his cozy burrow.

After paddling in the pond,
this duckling dozes in the tall, soft reeds.

After playing all day, you sleep in your snug little crib.

They are all getting bigger and bigger—

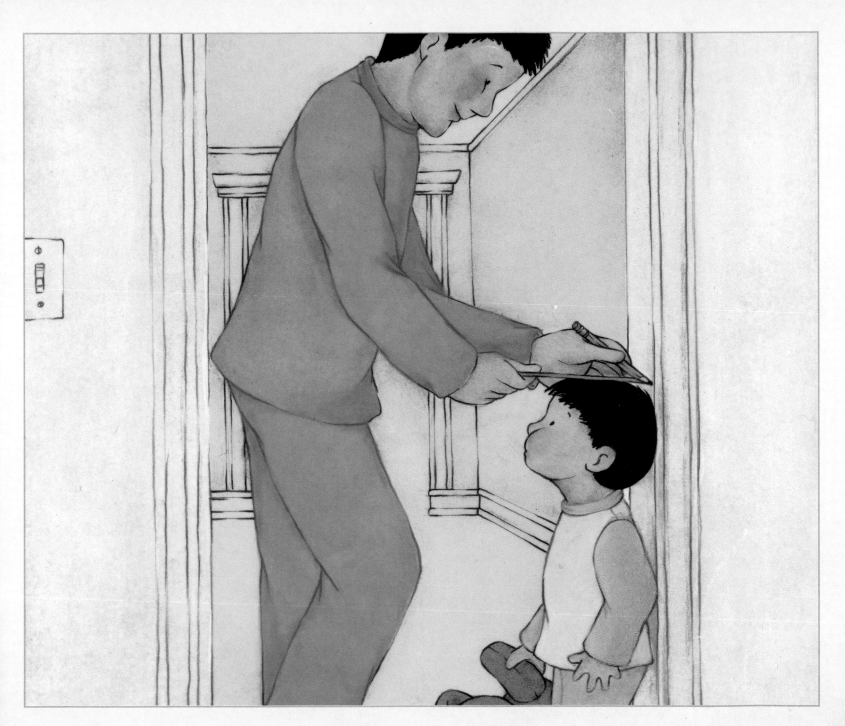

and so are you!

This foal has grown so big she now sleeps in her own stall.

This puppy sleeps in her new doghouse.

This kitten sleeps in his special basket.

And where will you sleep, now that you're big?

You'll sleep in your own big bed!

VIKING

Published by Penguin Group

Penguin Young Readers Group, 345 Hudson Street, New York, New York 10014, U.S.A.

Penguin Group (Canada), 90 Eglinton Avenue East, Suite 700, Toronto, Ontario, Canada M4P 2Y3

(a division of Pearson Penguin Canada Inc.)

Penguin Books Ltd, Registered Offices: 80 Strand, London WC2R 0RL, England

First published in 2008 by Viking, a division of Penguin Young Readers Group

5 7 9 10 8 6 4

LIBRARY OF CONGRESS CATALOGING-IN-PUBLICATION DATA

Bergstein, Rita M.

Your own big bed / by Rita M. Bergstein; illustrated by Susan Kathleen Hartung.

p. cm.

Summary: Introduces how different animals and even babies grow from being newly-hatched or born,

through being carried everywhere, to having their own special place to sleep.

ISBN 978-0-670-06079-5 (hardcover)

[1. Growth—Fiction. 2. Babies—Fiction. 3. Animals—Infancy—Fiction. 4. Beds—Fiction.] I. Hartung, Susan Kathleen, ill. II. Title.

PZ7.B452267You 2008

[E]—dc22

2007017902

Manufactured in China

Set in Excelsior

Book design by Nancy Brennan

*I would like to give my love and deepest thanks to my husband, Keith,
who encouraged my every step, and also to my three best girls
for being proud of their mom.*
—R.M.B.

For Ari—S.K.H.